Devon Holzwarth

Found You

ALISON
GREEN
BOOKS

This is Sami. His family just moved here.
Sami had lots of friends in his old home . . .

. . . but in this new place he keeps to himself. "Who did you play with today?" asks Mum.

But Sami only plays by himself.

He's
been
learning
to
juggle.

He doesn't
need friends
to juggle.

It's just that everything feels so different in this
new country. There's the lady on the bus who
always seems to be scowling at him.

And the baker who can't understand what his mum's trying to say.

And the girl at kindergarten, who laughs when he can only say his own name, and not much else.

Sami would rather hide than play with her.

Today he's at the park with his mum.
But this time he's not the only one
who's playing on his own.

High up in the trees, one little bird is
sitting apart from the rest. She seems to
be looking for something – or someone.

"Aha!" she chirps.
She zooms down, and . . .

BUMP!

. . . crashes straight into Sami.

Sami picks her up very gently.
"Are you okay, little bird?"

Little Bird
shakes her
feathers

and stretches
her wings.

"I think so," she says.
"But I'm lost. Can you
help me find my friends?"
"I'll do my best," says Sami. "I think
I saw some birds over by the swings."

The trees by the
swings are full of crows.
"Are these your friends?"

Little Bird shakes her head
– and stuffs her wings in her ears.
Those crows are really noisy!

Next Sami finds some pigeons.
"Are these your friends?"

Little Bird shakes her head sadly.

"Look!" whispers Sami.
"It's the old lady from the bus."

But she's not scowling today – in fact she
smiles at him, and gives him a handful
of grain so he can feed the birds, too.
"Thank you!" says Sami, shyly.
Little Bird helps herself as well.

Next they come to the pond.
Sami spots the baker, out on his lunch break.
He smiles and hands Sami a roll. There are ducks
and geese and swans and coots and they're
all really hungry. Sami tosses them
seeds from his roll.

"Are these your friends, Little Bird?"
he calls.

Little Bird shakes her head again.

"Don't be sad," says Sami. "I'm sure we'll find them soon."
Sami strokes her bright feathers –

– and suddenly remembers
where he's seen some birds just like her.
"The cherry trees, Little Bird!
That's where I saw your friends!"

But just as they're setting off, the girl
from Sami's kindergarten skips by.

She turns and catches his eye.
Sami gasps. His heart skips a beat.
What if she laughs at him again?

Before she can say a word, he scurries
off towards the cherry trees.

Little Bird pauses –

then follows him.

Little Bird's friends are very relieved to see her. **"There you are!"**

"Where were you?" they chirp.

"Why do you keep wandering off? It's time to go home!"

"Sorry," says Little Bird. "I had something important to do."

She dances around Sami.
"Thank you for helping me. You're
a very good friend."

"Am I?" says Sami.
He feels very proud.

He waves as the cloud
of birds lifts into the air.
"Bye-bye! See you soon!"
He feels so happy . . .

. . . until he realises that he's on his own again.

Sami's just wishing he could disappear when,
to his surprise, a ball rolls up . . .

. . . and the girl
from his class says,
"Will you play
with me?"

Sami doesn't know what to say.
Then he feels a fluttering by his
ear, and Little Bird whispers,
"Just say YES!"

Sami smiles, and . . .

. . . kicks the
ball right back!

Little Bird sighs with happiness.
Then she glances about her,
swoops off, and . . .

BUMP!

She crashes straight into a little girl
who's playing all by herself.

"Are you okay, little bird?"
Little Bird shakes her feathers and stretches her wings.
"I think so," she says. "But I'm lost. Can you help me find my friends?"

Heartfelt thanks to Zoë & Alison xo

First published in the UK in 2020 by
Alison Green Books
An imprint of Scholastic Children's Books
Euston House, 24 Eversholt Street
London NW1 1DB
A division of Scholastic Ltd
www.scholastic.co.uk
London – New York – Toronto – Sydney – Auckland
Mexico City – New Delhi – Hong Kong
Designed by Zoë Tucker

FOR JARED, MIRANDA & GRIFFIN ♥